Whale
Feels Worried

Franklin Watts
First published in Great Britain in 2021 by Hodder & Stoughton

Credits
Series Editor: Sarah Peutrill
Series Designer: Sarah Peden

ISBN: 978 1 4451 7457 0 (hardback)
ISBN: 978 1 4451 7458 7 (paperback)

Printed in China

Franklin Watts
An imprint of
Hachette Children's Group
Part of Hodder & Stoughton
Carmelite House
50 Victoria Embankment
London EC4Y 0DZ

An Hachette UK Company
www.hachette.co.uk

www.hachettechildrens.co.uk

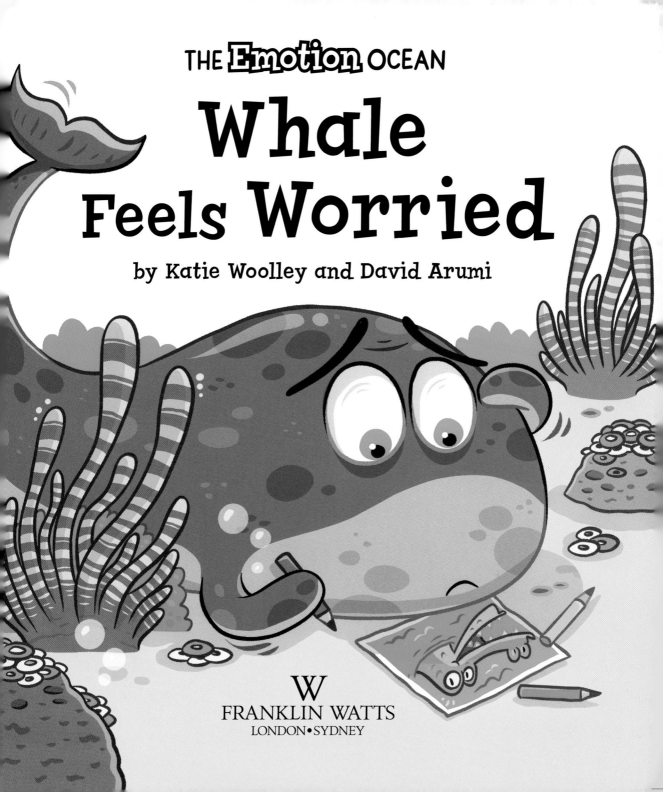

THE Emotion OCEAN

Whale
Feels Worried

by Katie Woolley and David Arumi

W
FRANKLIN WATTS
LONDON • SYDNEY

The animals of Class One were
busy drawing.

Angelfish finished quickly and swam outside to play.

Soon, all her friends joined in.

All except Whale, who was **worrying**.

Whale often felt worried. She worried that her tail fin was too big.

She worried that her skin was too bumpy.

Most of all, she worried about her schoolwork.

That night, Whale was still worrying.
It started out as a little worry, but her
worry **grew and grew.**

Whale wanted her picture of a snappy
crocodile to be perfect.

The next day, Whale felt glum.
Her worry was **huge!**

"Come and play!" shouted Starfish.

But Whale didn't hear her friend. She was too busy rubbing out her picture.

Suddenly, Whale rubbed so hard that she ripped it.

"Oh no!" she wailed. "I've ripped my crocodile!"

Whale burst into tears.

Just then, the bell rang.

"It's time to go in," said Starfish.
Whale didn't come.

Starfish picked up Whale's picture
and went inside.

Mr Narwhal came out to find Whale.

"Are you **okay?**" asked the teacher.

16

"I was so worried that my picture wasn't perfect, that I rubbed too hard," she wailed. "Now, it's **rubbish!**"

Mr Narwhal led Whale into the classroom.

"Worrying means you care, Whale," he said, "but it's okay to make mistakes."

"Is it?" whispered Whale. "Why?"

"Mistakes help us to learn," said Mr Narwhal. "There can be **beauty** in mistakes, too."

"Yes, there can!" laughed Shark. "We think this rip makes the **perfect** crocodile!"

A wide grin spread across Whale's face.
"It IS **perfect!**" she cried.

Then, Whale's face fell a little.

"What do I do when I have another worry?"
she asked.

"We all have worries sometimes," said Mr Narwhal. "Talking to someone can make a worry a little bit smaller."

"My worry does *feel* smaller," Whale whispered. "But it hasn't gone away."

25

"I have an idea," said Mr Narwhal.

The teacher got out a jar.

"This will be our class **worry jar**," he said. "If any of you has a worry, put it in here and it might help you stop thinking about it."

Whale wrote down her worry and put it in the jar. She did the lid up **extra** tight.

"How do you feel now?" asked Jellyfish.

Whale thought for a moment.

"I feel perfect!" she cried. "Come on! Let's play!"

Emotions are BIG!

Your feelings are a big part of you, just like they are a big part of Whale and her friends. Look at the pictures and talk about these feelings. Here are some questions to help you:

What was the thing that Whale worried about the most?

Why did Whale worry about her schoolwork?

What did Whale do to her picture?

What did Whale learn about making mistakes?

What did Mr Narwhal make to help the class make their worries feel a little smaller?

What could YOU do to understand a worry and make it feel smaller?

Let's Talk About Feelings

The Emotion Ocean series has been written to help young children begin to understand their own feelings, and how those feelings and subsequent actions affect themselves and others.

It provides a starting point for parents, carers and teachers to discuss BIG feelings with little learners. The series is set in the ocean with a class of animal friends who experience these big emotions in familiar, everyday scenarios.

Whale Feels Worried

This story looks at feeling worried, how it makes you feel, how you react to the feeling of being worried and what you can do to overcome the emotion.

The book aims to encourage children to identify their own feelings, consider how feelings can affect their own happiness and the happiness of others, and offer simple tools to help manage their emotions.

How to use the book

The book is designed for adults to share with either an individual child, or a group of children, and as a starting point for discussion.

Choose a time when you and the children are relaxed and have time to share the story.

Before reading the story:

• Spend time looking at the illustrations and talking about what the book might be about before reading it together.

• Encourage children to employ a 'phonics-first' approach to tackling new words by sounding them out.

After reading the story:

• Talk about the story with the children. Ask them to describe Whale's feelings. Ask them if they have ever felt worried. Can they remember when and why?

• Ask the children why they think it is important to understand their feelings. Does it make them feel better to understand why they feel the way they do in certain situations? Does it help them get along with others?

• Place the children into groups. Ask them to think of a scenario when somebody might feel worried. What could that person do to make themselves feel better? (For example, they could talk to a trusted grown-up or write down their worries in a diary.)

• At the end of the session, invite a spokesperson from each group to read out their list to the others. Then discuss the different lists as a whole class.